DATE DUE			
012890			
012389			
110701			
111401			
051702			

E
F
Mag

300BV00414591Q
Maguire, Arlene H.

We're all special

BAHIA VISTA SCHOOL
SAN RAFAEL,CA

326301 01186   36435C   003

WE'RE ALL
SPECIAL

Published by
PORTUNUS PUBLISHING CO. ©
3435 Ocean Park Blvd. Suite 203
Santa Monica, CA 90405

Copyright 1995 by Portunus Publishing ©
Artwork copyright by Sheila Lucas.
Text copyright by Arlene Maguire.
All rights reserved.
Printed in Hong Kong.
Third Printing: June, 1998

Design: EGRET DESIGN

Publisher's Cataloging in Publication
(Prepared by Quality Books Inc.)
Maguire, Arlene.
    We're all special/ Arlene Maguire.
    p.cm.
    ISBN 0-9641330-9-1
    1.Individuality--Children's literature.   2. Individuality.   3. Stories in
rhyme. I. Title.
    PZ8.3.M2727Were 1995   [E]
                                                              QB194-1867

This book is printed on recycled paper using soy ink.

WE'RE ALL SPECIAL

BY
ARLENE MAGUIRE

ILLUSTRATED BY SHEILA LUCAS

We're all special,

We're unique,

From the kind of clothes we wear

To the many ways we speak.

We come in many colors,

And shapes and sizes too.

We all have different interests

And different things we do.

Some folks love to garden,

They don't mind the bees,

While other folks discover

That the grass makes them sneeze.

Some like big cities,

Museums and a zoo,

Lots of excitement

And plenty to do.

Others like quiet,

In woods with tall trees,

A walk in the country

And a warm summer breeze.

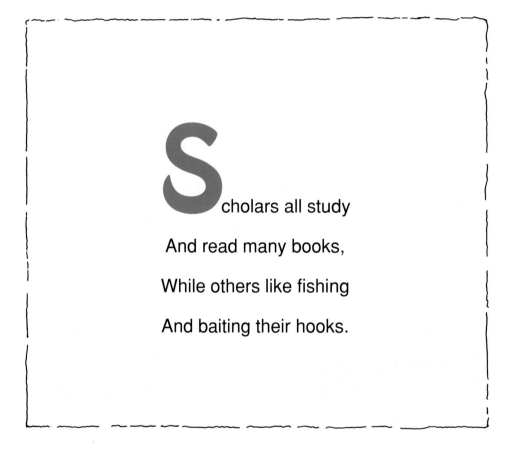

Scholars all study

And read many books,

While others like fishing

And baiting their hooks.

Some folks love racing

In boats and in cars,

While astronauts dare

To shoot for the stars.

Some folks are experts

On bugs and on snakes.

Some are mechanics,

They're experts with brakes.

One kid loves hamsters,

Another loves cats.

All kinds of people

Wear all kinds of hats.

Some folks are collectors

Of comics or shoes,

While others get rid of

The things they don't use.

A few folks love danger,

They love jungle hunts,

Climbing steep mountains

And high wire stunts.

Others sip tea

As they bathe in the sun,

Enjoying fine dining

And shopping for fun.

Yes, everyone's special

And likes different things.

One person will listen,

While someone else sings.

Some people are clever,

They win on quiz shows,

But love's more important

Than what someone knows.

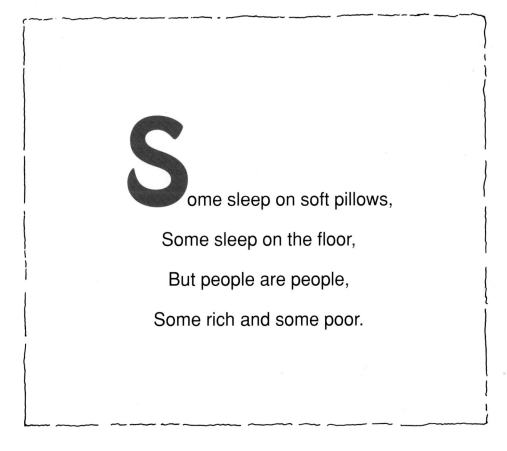

Some sleep on soft pillows,

Some sleep on the floor,

But people are people,

Some rich and some poor.

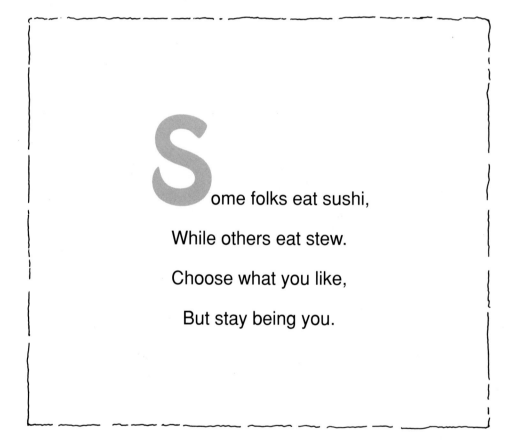

Some folks eat sushi,

While others eat stew.

Choose what you like,

But stay being you.

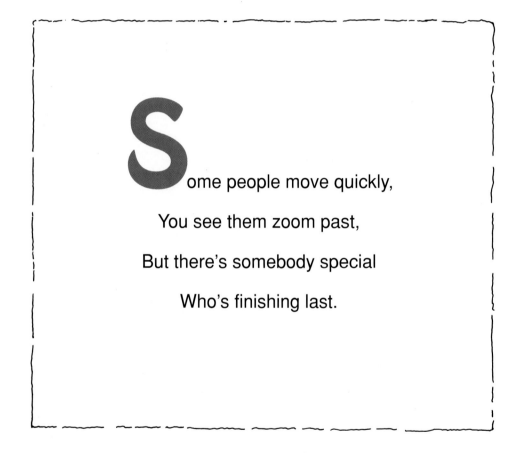

S ome people move quickly,

You see them zoom past,

But there's somebody special

Who's finishing last.

You really are important,

You are special and unique,

From the kind of clothes you wear

To the special way you speak.

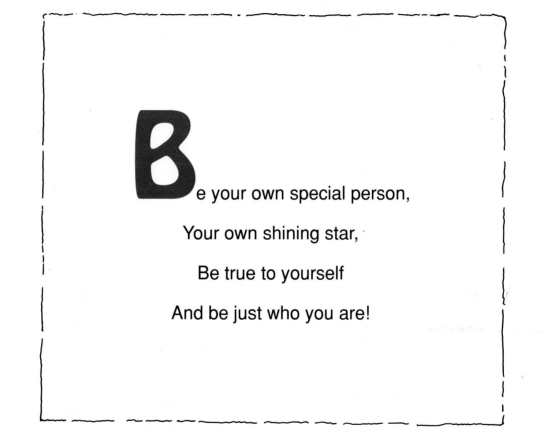

Be your own special person,

Your own shining star,

Be true to yourself

And be just who you are!